BIG CAT
Little Cat

Lisa Regan

BLOOMSBURY

LONDON DELHI NEW YORK SYDNEY

Published 2012 by
Bloomsbury Publishing Plc
50 Bedford Square, London, WC1B 3DP

www.bloomsbury.com

ISBN   HB 978-1-4081-6401-3
       PB 978-1-4081-8022-8

All photographs © Nature Picture Library and: p4, 10, 12, 14, 18, Anup Shah; p5, 7, Aflo; p6, Peter Blackwell; p8, Tony Heald; p9, 21, Adriano Bacchella; p11, Ulrike Schanz; p13, Mark Taylor; p15, Eric Baccega; p16, Suzi Eszterhas; p17, 19, Petra Wegner; p20, 22, Lynn M. Stone; p22 (inset), Jane Burton; p23, Mark Carwardine; p23 (inset), Michel Petit.

Manufactured and supplied under licence from the Zoological Society of London.

A CIP catalogue for this book is available from the British Library.

This book is produced using paper that is made from wood grown in managed, sustainable forests.

It is natural, renewable and recyclable. The logging and manufacturing processes conform to the environmental regulations of the country of origin.

Printed in China by C&C Offset Printing Co.Ltd.

HB   10 9 8 7 6 5 4 3 2 1
PB   10 9 8 7 6 5 4 3 2 1

FSC
www.fsc.org

MIX
Paper from responsible sources
FSC® C008047

Contents

Big cats like to take naps.

In the wild, big cats can sleep for up to 20 hours a day. They nap in the day because they hunt at night. Most big cats like to sleep on their own.

Cheetahs are the only wild cats that hunt for food during the day.

Lions often sleep together in **prides**.

Little cats nap too.

They can sleep up to 18 hours a day. Little cats also like to hunt for food at night.

Like big cats, little cats can see in the dark at night.

Big cats climb trees.

Big cats climb trees to hide from other animals or to hunt for food. Leopards sometimes store their food in trees to keep it away from other animals.

A leopard will often leave its food up in the tree for days and return only when it is hungry!

Of all the big cats, leopards are the strongest climbers.

Little cats sometimes mark their patch by scratching trees with their claws.

Little cats climb trees too.

They climb trees to look for food, or to hide from other, larger animals.

Big cat colours help them to hide.

The patterns on a big cat's fur match the colours and patterns around it, so it can disappear. A tiger's stripes look bright until they hide in long grass.

Big cats like lions and pumas that live in open spaces have plain fur, the same colour as rocks and dry grass.

The leopard's spots help it stay hidden in trees and bushes.

The most common patterns for little cats are stripes and blotches.

Little cats can hide too.

Their patterns keep them hidden while they creep up on a bird or a mouse.

Big cats have killer claws.

Their claws are sharp and curved, for catching and holding on to their food. All cats except cheetahs can pull in their claws to protect them. This means they can be quiet when creeping up on their **prey**.

A lion's claw can grow nearly as long as your finger.

Watch out for little cat claws too.

Pet cats use their claws for the same things: climbing, scratching, pouncing, hunting, and fighting off their enemies.

All cats need to scratch something hard to sharpen their claws.

Big cats have more than one baby.

Most big cat mums give birth to **several** babies at the same time. They usually have between two and four babies, called cubs. The babies are blind when they are born, and totally helpless.

Cats carry their babies by grabbing the loose skin at the back of the neck with their teeth.

A group of cubs born together, like these cheetahs, is called a litter.

Little cats have lots of babies too.

Baby pet cats are called kittens, not cubs. The mum feeds them with her milk and looks after them until they are safe on their own.

Pet cats usually have between two and five kittens.

Big cat babies love to play.

Cubs learn how to survive by playing with each other. They chase their brothers and sisters and fight with them. They are only having fun, but their sharp teeth and claws can still hurt!

Cubs practise pouncing on a moving object by jumping on their mum's tail as she flicks it on the ground.

The grown up lions stay patient as the cubs learn new tricks!

Kittens play with toys, just like children, and they get bored easily as well!

Little cats love playing too!

A kitten watches its mum to learn how to hunt. It tumbles and fights with other kittens for practice.

Big cats have superpowers!

Well – they do compared to humans. Their **senses** of hearing, sight and smell are much better than a person's. They can move their ears to hear sounds from far away. Some big cats can see six times better than us at night.

Big cats like this cheetah often turn their head instead of moving their eyes.

A cat blinks slowly, one eye at a time, so it can still see.

Little cats have good senses too.

They twitch their ears when they hear a tiny noise. Their sensitive nose picks up smells much better than a person can.

Big cats have sharp teeth.

They need to be extra sharp as big cats eat nothing but meat. They have long, pointed front teeth. These are for biting and killing. They also have special back teeth like knives, for tearing meat from bones.

A tiger has longer front teeth than any other cat.

Little cats have sharp teeth too.

Their teeth are not as big, but they are still very sharp! Little cats love meat, which is why they catch rabbits and birds.

Just like you, a cat has baby teeth that fall out to make room for its adult teeth.

Big cats have big whiskers.

A cat uses its whiskers to help it feel what is around it. The whiskers stick out to help the cat tell where it is, even in the dark. A tiger's face whiskers are about 15 centimetres long. A cheetah has shorter whiskers because it hunts in the daylight, so it can see more.

The whiskers on this clouded leopard grow out of black spots on the cheeks.

A cat's whiskers are much thicker than the rest of its hairs.

Little cats have long whiskers too.

Like big cats, a little cat uses its whiskers to help feel prey that is too close to its mouth to see properly.

Big and little cats aren't all the same.

Some, like tigers and jaguars, love the water and are good swimmers. They will catch prey in a river, and sit in shallow water to cool down.

Little cats often hate getting wet!

Cats make different sounds.

Lions, tigers, leopards and jaguars can roar but they can't purr. Other wild cats, like cheetahs and mountain lions, have different parts in their throat so cannot make the loud roaring noise.

Little cats can't roar, but they can purr.

Glossary

pride   a group of lions that live together

prey   an animal that is hunted and eaten by other animals

several   a few

senses   how the body knows what is going on around it – seeing, hearing, touching, tasting and smelling

About ZSL

The Zoological Society of London (ZSL) is a charity that provides help for animals at home and worldwide. We also run ZSL London Zoo and ZSL Whipsnade Zoo. By buying this book, you have helped us raise money to continue our work with animals around the world.

Find out more at **zsl.org**.